# VETERANS DAY

By ALLAN MOREY

Illustrations by GALIA BERNSTEIN

Music by MARK OBLINGER

**CANTATA**
LEARNING

11/2019

WWW.CANTATALEARNING.COM

# CANTATA
# LEARNING

Published by Cantata Learning
1710 Roe Crest Drive
North Mankato, MN 56003
www.cantatalearning.com

**Library of Congress Cataloging-in-Publication Data**
Names: Morey, Allan, author. | Bernstein, Galia, illustrator.
Title: Veterans Day / by Allan Morey ; illustrations by Galia Bernstein ;
  music by Mark Oblinger.
Description: North Mankato, MN : Cantata Learning, 2018. | Series: Holidays
  in rhythm and rhyme | Description based on print version record and CIP
  data provided by publisher; resource not viewed.
Identifiers: LCCN 2017007533 (print) | LCCN 2017012101 (ebook) | ISBN
  9781684100606 | ISBN 9781684100590 (hardcover : alk. paper)
Subjects: LCSH: Veterans Day--Juvenile literature.
Classification: LCC D671 (ebook) | LCC D671 .M67 2018 (print) | DDC
  394.264--dc23
LC record available at https://lccn.loc.gov/2017007533

978-1-68410-283-9 (paperback)

Book design, Tim Palin Creative
Editorial direction, Flat Sole Studio
Executive musical production and direction, Elizabeth Draper
Music arranged and produced by Mark Oblinger

Printed in the United States of America.
0390

ACCESS THE MUSIC!
SCAN CODE WITH MOBILE APP
CANTATALEARNING.COM

# TIPS TO SUPPORT LITERACY AT HOME

## WHY READING AND SINGING WITH YOUR CHILD IS SO IMPORTANT

Daily reading with your child leads to increased academic achievement. Music and songs, specifically rhyming songs, are a fun and easy way to build early literacy and language development. Music skills correlate significantly with both phonological awareness and reading development. Singing helps build vocabulary and speech development. And reading and appreciating music together is a wonderful way to strengthen your relationship.

### *READ AND SING EVERY DAY!*

## TIPS FOR USING CANTATA LEARNING BOOKS AND SONGS DURING YOUR DAILY STORY TIME

1. As you sing and read, point out the different words on the page that rhyme. Suggest other words that rhyme.

2. Memorize simple rhymes such as Itsy Bitsy Spider and sing them together. This encourages comprehension skills and early literacy skills.

3. Use the questions in the back of each book to guide your singing and storytelling.

4. Read the included sheet music with your child while you listen to the song. How do the music notes correlate to the words of the song?

5. Sing along on the go and at home. Access music by scanning the QR code on each Cantata book. You can also stream or download the music for free to your computer, smartphone, or mobile device.

Devoting time to daily reading shows that you are available for your child. Together, you are building language, literacy, and listening skills.

Have fun reading and singing!

Veterans Day is November 11. During this holiday, we thank the men and women who have served in the armed forces. People also visit national cemeteries to **honor** soldiers who have died. One of the best known is Arlington National Cemetery near Washington, DC. It is home to the **Tomb** of the Unknowns.

To learn what makes Veterans Day such a special holiday, turn the page and sing along!

Our president lays a **wreath**
at the Tomb of the Unknowns.
He shares a moment of peace.
He shares a moment of peace.

November 11th is Veterans Day.
It's time to watch America's Parade!

November 11th is Veterans Day.
It's time to raise an American flag.

It's Veterans Day.

We honor those who served.

We honor those who died.

We help those who were hurt.

We help those who were hurt.

November 11th is Veterans Day.
It's time to watch America's Parade!

November 11th is Veterans Day.
It's time to raise an American flag.

It's Veterans Day.

Veterans serve in peacetime.
They fight in times of war.

They fought in World War I,
World War II, and many more.

Soldiers keep us safe.
That's what they serve for.

November 11th is Veterans Day.
It's time to watch America's Parade!

November 11th is Veterans Day.
It's time to raise an American flag.

It's Veterans Day.

Our soldiers march with **pride**.

We stand up and salute them.

They hold their heads up high.

They hold their heads up high.

November 11th is Veterans Day.
It's time to watch America's Parade!

November 11th is Veterans Day.
It's time to raise an American flag.

It's Veterans Day.

# SONG LYRICS
## Veterans Day

Our president lays a wreath
at the Tomb of the Unknowns.
He shares a moment of peace.
He shares a moment of peace.

November 11th is Veterans Day.
It's time to watch America's Parade!
November 11th is Veterans Day.
It's time to raise an American flag.
It's Veterans Day!

We honor those who served.
We honor those who died.
We help those who were hurt.
We help those who were hurt.

November 11th is Veterans Day.
It's time to watch America's Parade!
November 11th is Veterans Day.
It's time to raise an American flag.
It's Veterans Day!

Veterans serve in peacetime.
They fight in times of war.
They fought in World War I,
World War II, and many more.
Soldiers keep us safe.
That's what they serve for.

November 11th is Veterans Day.
It's time to watch America's Parade!
November 11th is Veterans Day.
It's time to raise an American flag.
It's Veterans Day!

Our soldiers march with pride.
We stand up and salute them.
They hold their heads up high.
They hold their heads up high.

November 11th is Veterans Day.
It's time to watch America's Parade!
November 11th is Veterans Day.
It's time to raise an American flag.
It's Veterans Day!

# Veterans Day

**Children's March**
Mark Oblinger

**Verse**

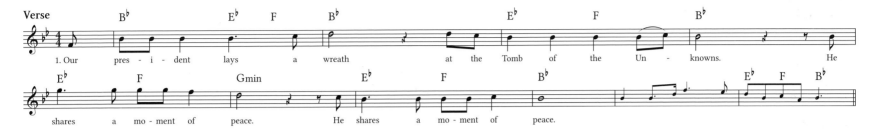

1. Our pres - i - dent lays a wreath at the Tomb of the Un - knowns. He

shares a mo - ment of peace. He shares a mo - ment of peace.

**Chorus**

No - vem - ber e - lev - enth is Vet - er - ans Day. It's time to watch A - mer - i - ca's Pa - rade! No - vem - ber e - lev - enth is

Vet - er - ans Day. It's time to raise an A - mer - i - can flag. It's Vet - er - ans Day!

**Verse 2**
We honor those who served.
We honor those who died.
We help those who were hurt.
We help those who were hurt.

**Chorus**

**Bridge**

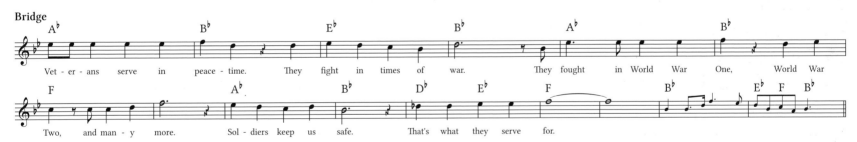

Vet - er - ans serve in peace - time. They fight in times of war. They fought in World War One, World War

Two, and man - y more. Sol - diers keep us safe. That's what they serve for.

**Chorus**

**Verse 3**
Our soldiers march with pride.
We stand up and salute them.
They hold their heads up high.
They hold their heads up high.

**Chorus**

# GLOSSARY

**honor**—to show respect and praise

**pride**—a feeling of satisfaction and self-respect

**tomb**—a grave, or a building for holding a dead body

**wreath**—flowers, leaves, and branches twisted together in the shape of a circle

# GUIDED READING ACTIVITIES

1. The American flag is red, white, and blue. Count how many white and red stripes it has. Can you count how many stars it has? Hint: there is one star for every state. Now draw a picture of an American flag.

2. Have you ever watched a parade? Was it for a holiday or other special event? What did you see in the parade? Were there soldiers marching?

3. Do you know anyone who has served in the armed forces? Ask them about their experiences, and be sure to thank them for their service!

## TO LEARN MORE

Dayton, Connor. *Veterans Day*. New York: PowerKids Press, 2012.

DeRubertis, Barbara. *Let's Celebrate Veterans Day*. New York: Kane Press, 2014.

Pettiford, Rebecca. *Veterans Day*. Minneapolis: Jump!, 2016.

Rissman, Rebecca. *Veterans Day*. Chicago: Heinemann Library, 2011.

# ONE HOT DAY

## A Tomás the Tortoise Adventure

Mike Miller

For Shelly, Jim, Molly and Matthew

For more Tomás adventures visit *www.tomasthetortoise.com*
Copyright 2004, Mike Miller and Stephens Press LLC

Written and illustrated by Mike Miller
Edited by Laura Brundige
Design production by Chris Wheeler and Digger Short

ISBN# 1932173-21-8

CIP Data Available

A *Las Vegas Review-Journal* Book

A Stephens Media Group Company
Post Office Box 1600
Las Vegas, Nevada 89125-1600

Printed in Hong Kong

Come On,
Let's Go!

In Red Rock Canyon
Where it's sunny and dry,
Tomás the tortoise
Opened one eye.

Naptime was over.
He wanted to play!
But the sand was too hot
At the end of the day.

It was well over 100
Outside his cave door.
He wanted to cool off
On a sandy lake shore.

He'd heard of Lake Mead,
Where Great-Uncle Ramón
Had once had a place
Where he'd lived all alone.

"I'll start off tomorrow!"
Tomás said, "Before light!"
He crawled back into his
hole to sleep for the night.

Very early next morning,
When the black sky turned rose,
Tomás set out, deciding
To follow his nose.

$H$e had walked for two hours
When footsteps came by.
He drew into his shell
Because he was shy.

"Yo, Tomás!" It was Chacko,
His coyote friend,
Who playfully rolled him
End over end.

He came bounding down
To see if Tomás was OK,
And Tomás informed him
There was no time to play.

"**I**'m off to Lake Mead
This bright sunny day!
Come along, Friend, and help me
Find the right way!"

And so they walked on
'Til they found in the sand
Luis the Lizard
Stretched out for a tan.

"We're going to Lake Mead!"
Tomás gave him a tap.
"Do you know the best way?
We don't have a map."

Luis jumped to his feet.
"I do know the route!"
I'll bring my sun screen
And some water, to boot!"

Then, over the hill,
With dust trailing behind
Burst Rapido Roadrunner:
"Hey there! Would you mind?

"I heard you three talking,
And I'd like to go
Right along with you
To the lake down below!"

So on the four headed
Along the long road,
Glad for the friendship
That lightened the load.

Late in the day
They decided to rest.
For tomorrow's adventures
They'd be at their best.

The sun went to bed,
But the sky was still bright;
Las Vegas lay twinkling
With dazzling light.

Tomás looked in wonder!
He thought it exquisite!
"Someday, when I'm older,
I'll go for a visit!"

On their way the next morning
They heard a strange grumbling.
"Oh . . . Ah . . . Oh . . . Oh!"
Somebody was mumbling.

It was Chico the Centipede,
Feeling the heat
Of the burning hot sand
On his hundred sore feet.

"Hop up on my back,"
Tomás said with a smile.
"I'll gladly carry you,
Every last mile."

Before long they came
To a very wide road.
Cars and trucks whizzed right past them
With big, heavy loads.

Crossing seemed hopeless!
The road was so wide!
How could they make it
Across from their side?

**W**ithout any warning,
Two hands grasped the shell
Of the frightened tortoise
Who had managed so well!

"Oh, no!" Tomás thought
As he tucked in his head,
"Some man has caught me!"
His heart fluttered with dread.

The traffic all stopped!
The man's sign told them to!
"Wow!" Tomás thought,
"The rumors weren't true!

"This human's not bad!
He helped us today!"
And so they continued
Toward the lake far away.

**J**ust over a rise,
Far over the hills,
They spied some dark clouds
Which gave Tomás chills.

**L**et's take the creek bed!
It's faster that way!"
Rapido was eager
To be on their way.

But Tomás was worried
And took the high trail.
He knew that flash flooding
Could cause them to fail.

Sure enough, soon came
A loud cry.
"The water is coming!
Get up where it's dry!"

hacko ran uphill
And then gave a shout:
"It's the dam!" he exclaimed,
"We're close! Have no doubt!"

Chacko was so thirsty
He ran on to the lake.
Rapido sped forward,
Leaving dust in his wake.

Chico jumped down
To hike on his own.
"Oh! . . . Ah! . . . Ooh! . . . Ow!"
He said with a groan.

Luis put on sun screen
He could see the water from here
Tomás plodded forward,
He knew they were near.

**D**own the last bank
They slid in a flash.
As they all hit the water
They made a huge splash.

omás was floating —
He looked like a boat.
Luis poured more sun screen
And began to float.

Rapido and Chacko
Tossed a beach ball.
The cold, clear, blue water
Delighted them all!

Chico was soaking
All one hundred hot feet.

This trip to the lake
Was a wonderful treat!

# The Desert Tortoise:

Desert tortoises can live to be 100 years old. Females normally lay 4 to 6 eggs during the month of June in a shallow hole and cover it with dirt. The eggs will take several months to hatch. Although they live in the desert, they stay in their burrows during the heat of the day and come out to graze on blossoms, plants and grasses during the early morning and evening hours. They hibernate during the winter in their burrows.